WALT DISNEY PRODUCTIONS
presents

The
Mystery Box

Random House  New York

Book Club Edition

First American Edition. Copyright © 1979 by The Walt Disney Company.
All rights reserved under International and Pan-American
Copyright Conventions. Published in the United States by
Random House, Inc., New York, and simultaneously in Canada
by Random House of Canada Limited, Toronto. Originally
published in Denmark as DEN MYSTISKE AESKE by
Gutenberghus Bladene, Copenhagen.
ISBN: 0-394-84358-4 (trade)   ISBN: 0-394-94358-9 (lib. bdg.)
Manufactured in the United States of America

7890   CDEFGHIJK

Huey, Louie, and Dewey were spending
a week with Daisy Duck.

The weather was terrible.

Daisy had waited all day for the rain to stop.

She wanted to go shopping.

Finally she said, "I cannot wait
anymore. I must buy
food for dinner before
the stores close."

Then she put on
her raincoat
and her scarf.

As Daisy was driving to town, she saw
an old woman walking in the storm.
She was carrying a large basket.

"That poor woman," thought Daisy. "I don't have much time, but I must offer her a ride." She stopped the car.

"Excuse me," said Daisy. "May I give you
a ride somewhere?"

"Yes, indeed," said the old woman. "Thank
you very much."

The old woman got into the car.
"Where may I take you?" Daisy asked.
"To the train station," said
the old woman.

The train station was
on the other side of town.
Daisy would be late
for her shopping.

They drove past the grocery store.
A sign on the door said, "Closed."
Daisy sighed.

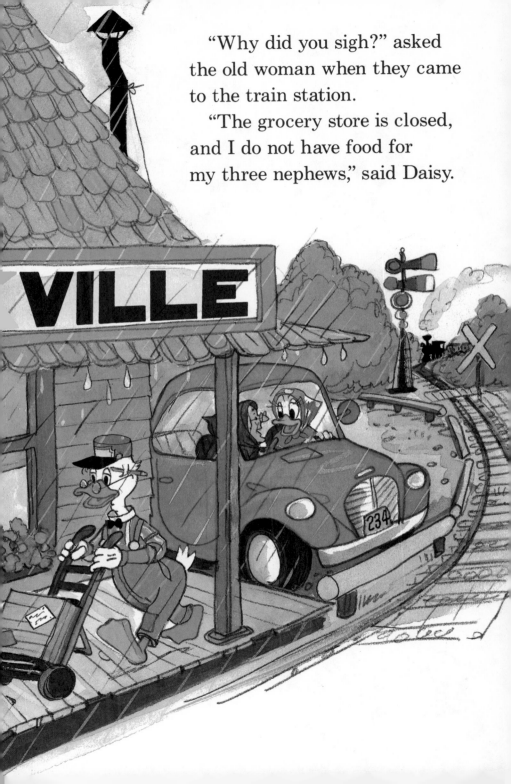

"Why did you sigh?" asked
the old woman when they came
to the train station.

"The grocery store is closed,
and I do not have food for
my three nephews," said Daisy.

"Take my basket," said the old woman.
"It is full of food. But there is a box
at the bottom which you must not open. I will
come for the box tomorrow when I return."

Daisy gave the old woman her address
and thanked her for the food.

By the time Daisy got home, the three boys
were very hungry.

"What is for dinner?" they asked.

"I do not know exactly," said Daisy.
"Whatever is in this basket."

Then she told them what had happened.

There was wonderful food
in the basket.

They found a big roast chick
and a jar of peaches...

ickled herring...

bread and cheese...

asparagus...

a bottle
of grape
soda...

apple pie...

fresh fruit...

and a red box that said,
"DO NOT OPEN!"

"This is a good dinner," said Huey.

"It sure is," said Louie.

"But I wish we could open
the mystery box," said Dewey.

"Well, we cannot,"
said Daisy.

"I will put the box away, so you will not think about it."

She put it on a high shelf in her closet.

Huey, Louie, and Dewey stayed up
late that night trying to figure out
what was in the mystery box.

They were still thinking about the box
the next morning.

When Daisy went out on an errand, they
decided to take a peek.

They stacked three chairs on top
of each other so they could reach
the top shelf of the closet.

Huey and Louie tried to hold the chairs
steady while Dewey reached in for the box.

CRASH!

The chairs slipped and fell.

Down came the three boys, Daisy's clothes, and the mystery box.

What a mess!
But the boys did not even notice
because now they had the box.

Then they heard a buzzing sound.
"Maybe it is a bomb!" said Louie.
"We should take it outside," said Huey.

When they were outside, they untied the string around the box and slowly lifted the lid.

"Help!" they cried. "Bees!"

Huey, Louie, and Dewey
all turned and ran.

They tried to hide, but
the bees found them.

Some of the bees flew down the street.
They chased Uncle Scrooge,
who had been mowing his lawn.
Then the bees found Ludwig Von Drake.
He swatted them with his rake.

Goofy the mailman came riding by.

When he heard the bees buzzing around him, he forgot to look where he was going.

He headed
right for Gus Goose,
who was painting
his house.

Goofy knocked Gus over
and spilled the paints.

Bzzzzz
Bzzzzz

The three boys were still running.
They came to a stream and tried
to cross it on an old log.

Bzzzzz

Bzzzzz

But the log didn't go all the way across.
At the end of it, the boys wobbled
and fell into the stream.

They stayed in the water until the bees
went away.

When Huey, Louie, and Dewey went back
to Daisy's house, they were wet and covered
with scratches.

They told Daisy what had happened.

"Oh dear!" said Daisy. "You should not
have opened the old woman's box."

"What will I tell
the old woman when she
comes?" said Daisy.

She was fixing the boys' scratches.
"We will tell her we are sorry,"
said Dewey.

Just then a taxi
stopped outside
the house.

"It is
the old woman!"
the boys cried.

The three boys told the old woman
what had happened.
And they said they were sorry.

"I must bring my bees back," said the old woman, pulling out a small gold whistle.

Bzzzzzzz *Bzzzzzz* *Bzzzzzzzz*

She played a little tune and the bees came and flew back into the box.

"Next time," said the old woman, "remember not to touch things that do not belong to you. Now I must go."

Then she turned and walked away.

Daisy was still angry with the boys. "The three of you will now go out and clean up the mess that you and the bees made," she said.

So Huey raked
Ludwig Von Drake's
lawn.

Louie finished
mowing the grass
at Uncle Scrooge's.

Dewey cleaned up the spilled paint
at Gus Goose's house.

And all three boys
ashed Goofy's
undry for him.

At the end of the week,
Uncle Donald came to get the boys.
Daisy baked a special cake.
"Well, boys, did you have a good time?"
Uncle Donald asked.

"Yes, we did," said Louie. "And
we learned a lot, too."
  "That's right," said Huey and Dewey.
  Daisy smiled and began serving the cake.